D0457834

PETER AND NED'S ULTIMATE TRAVEL JOURNAL

Written by Preeti Chhibber

Illustrated by George McClements and Stéphane Kardos

Designed by Catalina Castro

Los Angeles • New York

©2019 MARVEL

All rights reserved. Published by Marvel Press, an imprint of Disney Book Group.
No part of this book may be reproduced or transmitted in any form or by any means,
electronic or mechanical, including photocopying, recording, or by any information
storage and retrieval system, without written permission from the publisher.

For information address Marvel Press, 125 West End Avenue,
New York, New York 10023.

First Edition, June 2019

10 9 8 7 6 5 4 3 2

FAC-020093-19175

Printed in the United States of America

Designed by Catalina Castro

Cover illustration by George McClements and Stéphane Kardos

Library of Congress Control Number: 2018965992

ISBN: 978-1-368-04698-5

Visit www.DisneyBooks.com and www.Marvel.com

SUSTAINABLE FORESTRY INITIATIVE — Certified Sourcing
www.sfiprogram.org
SFI-00993

THIS LABEL APPLIES TO TEXT STOCK

Midtown School of Science and Technology

Dear Parent/Guardian:

Your child has been selected to join Midtown High School's History of Science Tour this summer. The chaperones will be **Mr. Harrington** and **Mr. Dell**. Please complete the following information and sign to allow your child to join.

I give my permission for **Peter Parker** to join **The History of Science Tour**, which includes stops in **Venice** and **Paris**.

Attached you will find the proposed itinerary, hotels, flight information, and chaperone contact information. Please make sure your emergency contact information is on file.

Comments/Concerns:

N/A

Signed **May Parker**

(Parent/Guardian)

HELLO AND WELCOME TO THE EPIC WRITINGS OF NED AND PETER!

Yeah, welcome! But what exactly are we writing, Ned?

Plotting? Memories? Schemes? Writing down great pickup lines for all the girls we're gonna meet in Europe?? Peter, the possibilities are endless, my child.

Why am I the child??

Because you're the one learning and going on missions and I'm the guy in the chair that tells you where to go.

. . . I guess that makes sense. Even though I don't know what you mean by missions, at all. No, sir. Also, it kind of sounds like someone's starting to enjoy his unlimited power a bit too much.

Touché, bud, touché.

Back to the journal. This is . . . our guide. Our guide to Europe. This is our totally awesome, totally normal European adventure journal.

It's weird when you say "totally normal" like that, Pete.

I'm just telling anyone who might read this over my shoulder (Hey, MJ!) that it is 100 percent average, normal, teenage-dude fun.

That doesn't sound
suspicious at all, Peter.

~~TOLD YOU!~~

Okay, sure, I can get on board with that.

That's why we're friends, Ned.

I'm your guy, Pete!

You guys are dorks.

Whatever, MJ, don't pretend like you don't love us.

WE'RE GREAT.

Wait, Peter, can we talk about you-know-who-with-the-you-know-webs? Web-head*? You know.

*How we refer to You-Know-Who

WHY WOULD WE DO THAT, NED?
I BARELY KNOW THE GUY.

But I ~~read in the newspaper~~ ~~heard on a podcast~~ read online that he's going to Europe this summer, too.

OMG,

you're **SO** bad at this.

6

THINGS TO DO BEFORE WE LEAVE THE COUNTRY

(Or, Peter and Ned are very unprepared and bad at packing)

Peter's Travel Check List

☐ Mini versions of everything: toothpaste, deodorant, soap.

So smol. So cute.

☐ Headphone splitter

Aw, do you wanna watch a movie with me, Parker?
That is <u>not</u> the plan
Right, the M—J plan.
That is not subtle.

☐ Clothes

☐ ~~Special Suit~~

☐ ~~"Contact" solution~~

I thought you got Lasik?
May must've added that . . .
Peter, aren't you forgetting something?

☐ **PASSPORT**

Ned's Travel Check List

☐ All the chargers, all the extra batteries

☐ My hat

> Hey, Ned, how many milliners does it take to make a hat?
>
> What's a milliner?
>
> It's a hatmaker—just guess, you're ruining the joke.
>
> This seems like a bad joke I'd tell. But okay, how many milliners does it take to make a hat?
>
> A million! Get it? Milliner? Million?
>
> Oh, buddy. That was really bad. And you know I love a good bad joke!
>
> I did it all for you, friend. We should call all these bad jokes NBJs for <u>Ned's Bad Jokes,</u> since you usually inspire them.

☐ Passport

☐ Business cards

> What? Why?
>
> Easiest way to get my contact info to the girls we're gonna meet, Pete!

☐ Clothes

☐ Nice clothes

> Are you bringing a tie, Pete?
>
> Yes ☹

PETER AND NED:
INTERNATIONAL MEN
OF AMAZINGNESS

Now that we have our passports, I looked up some of the sickest passport stamps online, and, Peter, we have to find these. We have to go.

Deal! What's on the list?

There is a place called the Polar Bear Capital of the World, and if we go, the passport stamp has a polar bear in it. I need this.

Well, then I want to go to

LLANFAIRPWLLGWYNGYLL-GOGERYCHWYRNDROBWLL-LLANTYSILIOGOGOGOCH

Wales, UK.

The town with the second longest name in the world? I'm familiar. *And I'm there.*

Do you think we could make it to Antarctica before these things expire? I'm pretty sure that would be a really awesome stamp to get.

Why not? What's stopping us?
I mean, other than not being grown-ups.

Not being grown-ups <u>right now.</u>

Did you guys know one of the most remote places in the world is this tiny island in the South Atlantic that takes five days to get to by boat from the closest port, because they don't have an airport? I want to go. Only like 300 people live there. It sounds amazing.

That sounds . . . safe.

I'd go with you, MJ.

Yeah, you WOULD, Pete.

So . . . Europe. That's a lot.

Advice and Notes from
Friends and Family!

Hey, Peter, I saw these texts on your phone and took screenshots and printed them and pasted them here. YOU'RE WELCOME.

Ned.

WHY?

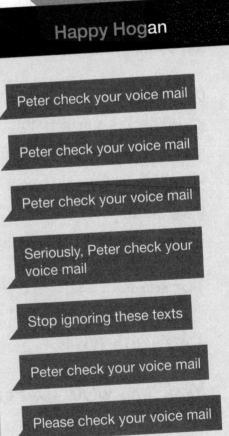

Happy Hogan

Peter check your voice mail

Peter check your voice mail

Peter check your voice mail

Seriously, Peter check your voice mail

Stop ignoring these texts

Peter check your voice mail

Please check your voice mail

Seemed helpful. Also because the Happy ones made me LOL IRL.

Glad <u>someone's</u> getting joy out of my harassment.

That's what friends are for!

Aunt May

Make smart choices, Peter! And don't forget to keep an eye out for trouble. You never know what you'll get pulled into overseas, so pay extra attention to your surroundings.

Quick vocab lesson.
Italian for help me: Aiutami
French for help me: Aidez moi!

I love you! Be safe! And please check in every night.

Notes from our chaperones!

Really? These, too?

I know! Such a good place to document these.

TO: science-euro-trip distribution group
FROM: MR. HARRINGTON
Subject: Good Vibes Only

Hey field trippers,

I don't know about you, but I am so excited for a trip out of the country with some of my favorite students. Just a reminder: let's keep it one hundred, as they say, and be polite to our European friends.

Don't forget that this trip is educational and starts the second the wheels touch the runway! In that spirit, for extra credit, make a list of things you wouldn't see on an American tarmac!

Please remember that we are meeting in front of security, not at the gate.

Let's go, Tigers.

Mr. Harrington

NBJ incoming! I hope I get to sit in an exit row so I can <u>exit this assignment</u>.

I'm glad you're leaning into the bad jokes, Ned.

TO: science-euro-trip distribution group
FROM: MR. DELL
Subject: Science Spots in Venice and Paris

Dear Students,

Please see the attached and list at least three exhibits/ attractions per item that you are excited to see. Also, while we're visiting these places, remember that you'll be expected to create an experiment inspired by the trip, so keep an eye out.

My personal favorite is Leonardo da Vinci's Bridge of the Golden Horn, just something to consider.

Mr. Dell

Attachment: SCIENCE TRIP.DOC

Mr. Dell's Science Itinerary

VENICE

Museo Leonardo da Vinci

Fondaco dei Turchi

Science and Secrets of the Lagoon Tour

> *Peter, it sounds like there could be monsters on this tour!*
>
> *Maybe I'll skip that day.*

PARIS

Musée de l'Homme

> *Museum of the Man—heck yeah!*
>
> *I don't think this is going to be what you think it's going to be.*

Palais de la Découverte

> *This one has a Pi Room, where they pi to the 707th digit and I can't wait to see it.*

Galerie de Minéralogie et de Géologie

> *NERD!*
>
> *We're both nerds.*
>
> *Oh yeah. Nerds are cool.*
>
> *Yeah, they are.*

La Cité des Sciences et de l'Industrie

```
        DELMAR'S DELI
         QUEENS, NY
           11238
        (712) 555-0111


   FOR DELIVERY: Peter Parker


2 Face Mask ............................... 2.99/e

1 4-Pk Tooth Brsh Caps ................ .99/e

10 ChocoChoco Bar ...................... .99/e

5 Salteez Pk .................................. .50/e

5 Sour Gamz Pk ............................ .50/e

TAX ............................................... 2.56


TOTAL ...................................... 24.43
```

Mr. Delmar seriously judged my purchase. It's not like I'd rather eat junk food than delicious Italian pasta!! We need plane snacks!

We really do. Growing boys cannot survive on packs of pretzels alone. Oh, and thanks for picking up those face masks, the plane's a great place for skin care, Pete. Gonna be smoooooooooth when we land in Venice. And this is a mask you can wear! I mean, not that you're used to wearing masks.

NED.

VOICE MAIL TRANSCRIPTS FROM NICK FURY

Ned, stop eavesdropping.

But you put it on speakerphone . . .

Wait, don't write this down, Ned!

But it could be important! And don't you want to remember when THE Nick Fury called you??? It's only the coolest thing ever!

- - - - - - - - - - - - - - - -

Voice Mail 1: Peter Parker, this is Nick Fury. Yes, _that_ Nick Fury. I need you to call me back immediately. You can reach me at

-VOICE MAIL DELETED-

Nope, no thank you, not right now, I am very busy.

Uh . . . is it okay that you . . . deleted this?

Voice Mail 2: Parker, it's Fury. I think maybe you accidentally deleted my last message. Call me back. NOW.

HE KNOWS WHAT YOU DID
I DIDN'T DO ANYTHING!

- - - - - - - - - - - - - -

Voice Mail 3: Parker, do not delete this. Contact me immediately.

Oh my God, can he see us???

...I don't think so????

- - - - - - - - - - - - - -

Voice Mail 4: Kid, you have to know that you're going to talk to me. There's no getting around it. No, I promise you. There's no getting around it.

Now I think he can <u>hear</u> us, Peter.

Voice Mail 5: Parker, I'm giving you one hour to call me back.

Oh, man, this is not good.

This is definitely not good.

Kinda feels like your Ole Parker Luck is rearing its ugly head.

Oh no, it is. It is my Ole Parker Luck following us to Europe.

That Ole Parker Luck: When an International former head of S.H.I.E.L.D. won't stop calling you because he wants you to be a Super Hero even though you're on vacation?

...Maybe this is a **NEW** kind of that Ole Parker luck.

THAT OLE PARKER LUCK:

Every time something bad happens that only happens because my name is Peter Parker and I have the worst luck.

PETER AND NED'S RULES FOR SHARING A ROOM

Let's get these down before we even leave because you know when we get to Europe we're going to be way too tired to make important decisions, like who gets to shower first.

1. He who makes it in the door first gets to pick the bed he wants.

   That's not FAIR, and you know why, Pete.

   There have to be <u>some</u> perks!

2. If you have to fart, go to the bathroom.

   Look, I thought your spidey-sense would warn you.

   That's not the point, the room <u>still</u> smells.

3. Don't borrow the other person's suit.

It was one time, Pete. You have to let it go.

4. You know what, be careful when touching any of Peter's things because how was I supposed to know those glasses were special when they just look like glasses.

5. Don't make "I told you so" faces at your best friend.

6. Peter Parker is not allowed to say anything ever.

That seems unfair, Ned.

I didn't make the rules.

You literally wrote that down. You are literally writing the rules right now!

7. Wait, what about the shower? I want to shower first. I call dibs.

Great, then I'll sleep in.

8. Peter gets to sleep in while Ned showers first.

Joke's on you! I'll shower at night!

9. Anyway. Please do not lose your room key. We only get two. Probably. I don't know how European hotels work. Do they just have big brass keys for their rooms? Wait, are we going to stay in a castle?

Lol did you forget Mr. Harrington booked our hotel?

Noooo! I didn't know I wanted to stay in a castle until just now!

FLIGHT ITINERARY

AIR USA

JOHN F. KENNEDY INTERNATIONAL AIRPORT > VENICE MARCO POLO AIRPORT
FLT # US174 TERMINAL 4 GATE B39
Parker, Peter Seat 24B
Leeds, Edward Ned Seat 24A

Hey, Ned, if we're on a flight and you're helping me with MJ does that make you my wingman? #NBJ

HOW TO SPEND THE DAY TRAVELING WITH YOUR BEST FRIEND

Or, the coolest games we've invented

A list of games in no particular order that will pass all the time:

SELFIE DEATH STARE

This one is easy. Make the worst face you can and take a selfie, show it to the other person, and if they laugh they lose.

> Ned cheats at this game.
>
> You can't cheat in Selfie Death Stare!
>
> You totally cheat. NO LIPS is cheating.
>
> No Lips is _not_ cheating.

Instructions for No Lips, aka the funniest face a person can make:

1) Make sure your lips are really, really dry.

2) Roll your bottom lip down so it's stuck against your teeth. Now do the same for your top lip with your top row of teeth.

3) Open your eyes wide, and try to smile.

4) Peter Parker will laugh so hard he pees his pants.

I am **never** telling you anything ever again. 😑

It was ONE time!! 😊 😊

I'm gonna tell Spider-Man to never bro hug you ever again.

Worth it, bro.

MORE GAMES! ⟶

TOP THAT

Pick a category (food, movies, whatever) and then try to one-up the other person's version of what that thing is.

Burrito

Hand-Wrapped Gift from God

The Mail-Order Delivery System for Meat and Cheese

Weather Reports Soft Clouds with a Chance of Spicy Meats and Queso

- - - - - - - - - - - - - - - -

Lamp

Glowing sphere of warmth

Electric glass ball that packs the heat

Luminous scientifically-sound orb that emits beams of radiance

Horse

Four-legged king of the fields

Majestic animal transportation system too good for us silly humans

Creature of beauty and dignity, who goes by the name Mr. Ed

- - - - - - - - - - - - - - - - - -

Spider-Man

Ned!

Not Ned, Spider-Man.

Ugh, fine. Arachnid Homo sapien

Eight-legged man insect monster

He doesn't have eight legs! And spiders aren't insects!

Arachno-boy!

Games we are going to figure out how to code into our TI-89 calculators:

-BOWLING

-SKIING

-SPACE FIGHTS!

-PUNCH'EM

-FOOTBALL

BEST MOVIES TO WATCH ON THE PLANE

1. Science Fiction

   Easy. It's exciting, and will distract you from the, you know, being-40,000-feet-in-the-air thing with the crashes and the booms and the aliens.

2. Cartoons

   Lull you into the sense of happiness you had when you were little. How could you not feel good listening to lions and mermaids sing?!

3. Documentary

   Pick up tips for our internet videos! Also, it's kind of cool the random things people decide to make movies about.

   Did you watch the one about the haunted Italian villa???

   Yes! So creepy and great! I probably won't have nightmares...

   ~~Too bad you guys couldn't watch it together, huh.~~

4. Anime

Cool fight scenes! And those sound effects. And they're so pretty.

5. Comedies

You just have to be careful not to laugh too loudly or it turns out the people behind you will complain and then the flight attendant will tell your teachers. ☹

6. Fantasy

This is only low on the list because sometimes you have to pay really close attention to the movie, and that's hard when the pilot keeps interrupting with announcements or whatever. We get it. We're _flying_, it might get bumpy.

7. Drama/Romance

Nope! Life is too short!

MJ'S RECOMMENDED PLANE READS

1. Between the World and Me by Ta-Nehisi Coates

2. American Street by Ibi Zoboi

3. Narrative of the Life of Frederick Douglass by Frederick Douglass

4. "The Cask of Amontillado" by Edgar Allan Poe

5. The House of the Spirits by Isabel Allende

Wow, MJ, these all sound awesome!

Enjoy your cartoons, kids

ROMANCE REC FROM NED

Do your best friend a favor and end up sitting next to someone you didn't even know was the girl of your dreams!

BETTY BRANT!

My one and only ♥

I'm glad this worked out for you, bud.

Peter, I can see you staring at MJ. Maybe you can sit next to her on the boat on the way to the hotel!

I hope so.

HOW TO DISTRACT YOURSELF WHEN YOU END UP SITTING NEXT TO AN OVERSHARING TEACHER FOR AN ENTIRE PLANE RIDE

By Peter Parker

Dude, this is that **OLE PARKER LUCK** *if I ever saw it.*

- Put your headphones in, but keep nodding and smiling.

- Pretend to be very interested in the in-flight magazine.

- **SLEEP.**

- Don't get sucked into the story.

- Definitely don't agree when he starts talking about his ex-wife.

- Oh no, his ex-wife faked her own death in the Battle of New York...

- Oh man, that is SO sad.

- Mr. Harrington, no.

- Mr. Harrington, <u>why</u>.

- Wait, don't get sucked in!

- Go to the bathroom every time the conversation starts again.

- Pretend there's a line for the bathroom even if there isn't one.

- Be "polite" and keep letting people go ahead of you in the fake bathroom line.

- Make eye contact with Mr. Dell and know that he knows your pain.

- Keep getting up to "stretch your legs."

- Get distracted by MJ and Brad sitting together.

- Sit with Mr. Harrington and be sad with him.

Hey, Pete, did you know Venice is called "The Sinking City"? Why are we going here again????

Because Mr. Harrington wanted to, and Mr. Dell is obsessed with science.

At least if it sinks, I can go knowing that I met the love of my life on this plane.

Okay, Ned.

How was sitting with Mr. Harrington, anyway? It looked brutal.

It <u>was</u> brutal. But he's got a lot going on. I get it.

At least you didn't have to sit next to Flash.

Even the Ole Parker Luck doesn't hate me <u>that</u> much!

Just enough to watch Brad and MJ, huh?

I know, buddy. But hey. Venice! The city of love!

That's **Paris**, Ned.

It's wherever your heart is true, Peter. Trust me.
I'm just glad we made it to Venice, I mean, we just
flew all the way from New York and BOY ARE MY
ARMS TIRED.

THE NBJ
STRIKES WHEN
YOU NEVER
EXPECT IT!

THINGS NOT TO DO WHEN YOU'RE HAVING A CONVERSATION WITH A CUSTOMS AGENT IN A FOREIGN COUNTRY

Starring Peter Parker, written by Ned Leeds

A note by its star: "My aunt put the suit in my bag and it surprised me and so I was very nervous, and that is my only excuse."

OKAY, AND NOW . . .

SCENE

Int.: Venice Marco Polo Airport

GROUPS OF KIDS MILL OUTSIDE OF CUSTOMS WAITING FOR PETER PARKER [MALE, 16, PRETTY AVERAGE-LOOKING GUY]

HEY!

[Okay, good-looking guy, I guess, who appears nervous and awkward at the window of a very bored-looking customs agent]

PETER
Ha-ha, here's my passport.

CUSTOMS AGENT
Do you have anything to declare?

PETER
I declare that I am excited about being in Venice!

CUSTOMS AGENT LOOKS UP FROM HIS SCREEN AND STARES AT PETER.

CUSTOMS AGENT
Oh, a funny American?

PETER
No, no, sorry, just nervous about traveling.

CUSTOMS AGENT
Why are you nervous? Are you hiding something?

PETER
What? No! No, I'm just. Sorry, I was just—

PETER'S VOICE DROPS TO A WHISPER.

PETER
Kidding.

CUSTOMS AGENT ROLLS HIS EYES AND
STAMPS PETER'S PASSPORT.

CUSTOMS AGENT
Well, this is serious business. So, no kidding. I think
we'll need to look at your bag, Mr. Parker.

AND THEN . . .

THEY GOT MAD ABOUT AN AMERICAN BANANA. THAT OLE PARKER LUCK STRIKES AGAIN.

THINGS MR. HARRINGTON HAS SAID THAT HE <u>THINKS</u> ARE ITALIAN, WHAT THEY <u>ACTUALLY</u> MEAN, AND WHAT I <u>THINK</u> HE MEANT:

Mr. Harrington:

Ciao, siamo di New York, cosa sono le auto?

Translation:

Hello, we are from New York, what are cars?

What he probably meant:

Hello, we are from New York, where are the taxis?

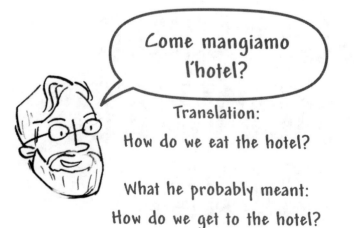

Come mangiamo l'hotel?

Translation:

How do we eat the hotel?

What he probably meant:

How do we get to the hotel?

Translation:
Your trash is very nice.

What he probably meant:
You have a lovely home.

- - - - - - - - - - - - - - - - - - -

Mr. Harrington:
Questa stanza odora di fuoco!

Translation:
This room smells like fire!

What he probably meant:
This room smells like flowers!

Hey, MJ, how do I say "bae" in Italian??

MJ, do <u>not</u> tell him.

OKAY, a quick Italian lesson.

English: I'm lost.

Italian: Mi sono persa.

English: Help me.

Italian: Oh! I know this one! **Aiutami.**

And the very coolest Italian word there is, *boh.*

What's that mean?

It's like "get out of my face" or "I don't know."
It's like . . . the perfect word.

English: Spider-Man

Italian: L'Uomo Ragno

Ha, why do you know how to say Spider-Man in Italian?

Seemed like something we should know. BOH.

Mr. Dell does NOT
find Mr. Harrington
amusing and it is
HILARIOUS.

TOP THINGS TO DO IN VENICE

(Based on five minutes of internet research)

(Maybe, like, seven minutes of internet research)

"Honestly, with all the dead-end alleyways and bridges, you're definitely going to get lost. So you may as well enjoy it!" Seen on the cover of a brochure at the airport

This sounds like so many bad things waiting to happen and I just want to relax omg.

ST. MARK'S BASILICA

It seems like there are a lot of basilicas in Venice. What is a basilica??

A big building, I think?

ST. MARK'S CLOCK TOWER

I bet there's a great view from the top of this thing.

If only we knew someone who could get up there to get great pictures.

DOGE'S PALACE

Much old.

Very art.

Wow. Such guild.

Many chamber.

Very tourist.

I knew you liked memes!

WALKING TOUR OF THE GRAND CANAL

Is this supposed to say boating tour? It's a canal. Of water.

CÀ DEL SOL

YES! These masks are so cool.

AND SCARY!

But totally also cool. Like, so cool.

BOAT TOUR OF VENICE

See, this makes more sense.

Peter, there are places to walk in Venice. You know that, right?

Yeah! Yeah, I knew that. I totally knew that.

He definitely didn't think Venice was all underwater. Because I didn't say that it was. That's for sure.

VENICE GONDOLA RIDE AND SERENADE

Ned, tell me you didn't.

Oh, I did. Me and Betty. NETTY ON THE WATER! GET READY!

NETTY?

Netty: You know me and Betty had to have a wicked couple name.

PONTE DI RIALTO

Venice also has so many bridges.

Well . . . it's a city of canals, buddy.

I <u>know.</u> I wish some of our bridges in New York looked like the bridges here, though. So cool. This bridge has been around since the 12th century. Well, sort of.

Sort of?

It's fallen down and been rebuilt five times?

Note to self: Stay off bridges in Venice. Boat travel only.

PIZZA! PASTA!

There are food tours. We can go on a FOOD TOUR!

Why isn't this at the top of the list???

Food is a really important part of culture, but something tells me that's not what you guys are excited about.

Lies! It's totally for culture!

And carbs! And cheese!

Cà Del Sol: Gift for MJ??? Mask??? Murano glass?? It's so shiny—maybe she'd like it??

MJ'S ITINERARY FOR VENICE

This is where things will <u>really</u> get good.

CEMETERY ISLAND

That's dark, MJ.

I know, right? It's going to be awesome.

A CRIME TOUR OF OLD VENICE

Do you know how many murder mysteries there are in Venetian history? This is going to be so cool.

Why do you know how many murder mysteries there are in Venetian history?!

THE HORSE STATUES OF SAN MARCO

These statues were stolen <u>multiple</u> times! The originals are in the basilica, but the fake ones are still displayed outside.

THE BRIDGE OF SIGHS

Wow, this sounds really pretty.

Lord Byron wrote that it was where convicts would see one last beautiful view of the city before . . . you know.

. . . Being freed for being imprisoned by accident?

Oh, Peter, you're cute.

UMMMMMMM...

This is sort of like their plague tour.

Their <u>what</u>?

Mwha ha ha ha.

THE VENETIAN HOME OF NIETZSCHE

"When I seek another word for 'music,' I never find any other word than 'Venice.'"

–Nietzsche

MJ, don't you want to go anywhere that has, like, cool stores?

Nah, I'm good.

She's good!

Boh.

♥*AN ODE TO BETTY BRANT*♥

By *Ned*, and definitely **NOT** BY PETER

Shall I compare thee to a summer's day
> You can't steal lines from other poems!
> It's called an HOMAGE

No, I'll compare thee to Shakespeare . . .
> . . . Ned, you're not!

. . . 's first sonnet
Which took the world by storm
Just like you took my heart
> This poem is taking the contents
> of my stomach.

You are so smart, I call you bae
And I know that you will say
It back to me
Because we are perfection
Hand in hand together
> Perfection? Are you sure you want
> to use the word perfection?
> YES, PETER, WHY WOULDN'T I?

Your face is like a perfect Queens sunset

        Smoggy and smelly?

Pink and perfect, and I bet

You don't even try

Your style and beauty

Are effortless, my queen, you slay

        Ned. **NED.**

        I'm begging you, don't give this to her.

NED'S VENETIAN ROMANCE RECOMMENDATION:

Take a gondola ride and write her a poem! It'll work every time!

(Or once, it'll work once. Because that is how many times it has worked. I can't believe that poem worked.)

PRETTY EVENTFUL FIRST DAY IN EUROPE

So, first impressions of Venice. I don't understand why this city already hates me? I got held up at customs, fell in the Grand Canal, and had some random dude show me up fighting a water demon monster thing???

You have to admit that fight was <u>so awesome</u>, though. Right? Like, that guy had a cape. And so many flashes! You should let this Mysterio dude handle this stuff, anyway. Because it seems like he really knows what he's doing, right? I mean, he's a grown-up.

Yeah, that's true. And I didn't really want to have to, you know, suit up while we're over here. So, great, go to town, Mysterious Mysterio!

60

Did you figure out what you wanted to get MJ?

Yes! I found the <u>perfect</u> thing. She's going to love it.

. . . Well?

I don't want to jinx it, so you'll have to wait and see.

But I can tell you if it's good or not. I mean, I'm in <u>love</u> now.

LOVE. Uh-huh.

TRUE LOVE!

Sure.

Pete, is it just me or does it feel like our hostel is sinking?

It might be sinking.

That reminds me. Today's Saddest Thing We Heard Mr. Harrington Say:

This hostel reminds me of my apartment.

LEONARDO DA VINCI MUSEUM'S BEST INVENTIONS

Mr. Dell says that Leonardo da Vinci is considered the first modern scientist.

Peter, why did it feel like all the paintings could see into my soul??? Also, Leonardo was <u>scary</u> good at drawing the inside of people.

Dude, I know. I felt like there were a thousand eyes watching us. So creepy. And why <u>was</u> he so good at drawing the inside of people?

I was very impressed by all of the wooden replicas based off of Leo's drawings. Particularly the one of the bicycle. Did Leo invent the bicycle??

Follow-up question: Could we get our hands on a time machine?

I liked the one that looked like a dome.

Was that a space shuttle? It looked like a wooden space shuttle with a bunch of gears in it. I'm 90 percent sure that Leonardo da Vinci was a time-traveling demon.

It's not like weirder things don't exist.

So true, Pete, so true.

- - - - - - - - - - - - - - - - - - -

Oh, that was the bridge Mr. Dell was talking about!

We're in Venice—of course it's a bridge.

Be honest, Ned, how many tries did it take you to build your own model afterward?

- - - - - - - - - - - - - - - - - - -

Who needs webs when they could have paper wings!

That doesn't seem like a good trade.

- - - - - - - - - - - - - - - - - - -

One of the replicas looked like a very early version of a soccer ball?

I think you mean a <u>football</u>, Ned.

That sounds like an NBJ, bud.

— — — — — — — — — — — — — — — — — —

I liked the one that looked like a way to shoot people into the sky for some reason?

Ha-ha, definitely a way to get a burrito into my mouth from the other side of a football field.

No, no, it's a way for us to send Flash over to his flashmob fans back home!

— — — — — — — — — — — — — — — — — —

Okay, so that scale-looking thing was the machine that they'll use TO MEASURE THE WEIGHT OF OUR SOULS.

AND WILL NOT BE FOUND WANTING! MWHA HA HA.

Guys, it was a hygrometer. It measures the humidity in the air. Wish it was souls, though.

MICHELANGELO VS. LEONARDO

...AND GO!

Michelangelo, all the way! Sistine Chapel? The <u>David</u>? That one statue that is in the Vatican?

What?? FIRST: How do you know so much about artists from the Italian Renaissance? SECONDLY, Leo was a genius.

FIRST: Rude, I am very smart and very interesting. And maybe my aunt made me watch a 1970s movie starring some old dude as Michelangelo when I was eight and it imprinted on my brain. And second: So was Mike! Let me say again, the <u>DAVID</u>.

I can't believe THIS is the thing you're going to fight with MJ about, Pete. THIS.

You went to the museum, Peter. Look at all the things he invented. And you can't just keep saying "David" in response to everything I say.

Okay, I'm not saying Leo wasn't great. But Michelangelo made actual sculptures out of marble, before power tools were invented, that look like they're ALIVE.

So do Leo's paintings!

I feel like it's harder to make a whole sculpture than a painting, though.

OMG. He made *perfect* paintings.

He made amazing paintings. But, like, Michelangelo has multiple iconic pieces. Leo's got...the <u>Mona Lisa</u>?

And the <u>Last Supper</u>!

Lol, oh sorry, I meant two iconic pieces.

I'm going to leave you now.

SPIDEY'S LIST OF BEST VENETIAN FOODS TO EAT WHILE SWINGING AROUND THE CITY

Narrated by Spider-Man himself to Ned through an open window like a weirdo

1. FRIED FOOD IN A PAPER CONE

It really doesn't matter what's in the cone, just that it's fried, am I right?? A fritter, cheese, whatever you want. Put that in a cone so I can put my face in it.

2. GELATO (in a cone)

That's two cone-shaped foods in a row, but they fit in my hand really well. And gelato is just ice cream, but creamier and better. Pro tip: Don't ask for a "scoop" because Italians don't use scoops. They use spades and it is way cooler, too.

3. PIZZA!!

What else do I need to say? It's pizza. Italian-style pizza. It's a little messy, but every food can be eaten on the go if you try hard enough. I am going to mention that it's better to do this _after_ crime fighting than before, because sometimes having a food baby in your belly will come back to haunt you in the middle of a fight.

4. STROMBOLI

Yum! We have these in Queens, too. This is basically pizza but rolled up: bread, sauce, cheese, all in a conveniently rolled-up, portable packet. Also, I can hang upside down and eat this and nothing falls out! (Then Spidey did a chef's kiss.)

5. PANZEROTTO

This is a teeny, tiny smol calzone and I am in love with it. A teeny, tiny adorable pocket of . . . cheese. How could I not be in love? We're getting married. Don't worry, I'll send you all invitations.

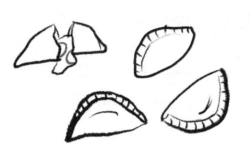

REASONS NED IS A GREAT FRIEND:

He will take a tranquilizer dart to the neck courtesy of NICHOLAS FURY and not complain about it. Because why would I complain when it is easily the COOLEST THING THAT HAS EVER HAPPENED TO ME??? PETER, NICK FURY WAS IN OUR HOTEL ROOM.

I can't believe this is happening, oh my God. How am I going to keep this a secret from Betty????

Ned, you cannot tell her!

I know, I know, but oh man, this is huge.

THIS. IS. HUGE.

Secret identity, Ned.
Key word being: SECRET.

S-E-C-
R-E-T!

But you're not going to . . . go with him, are you? It sounds dangerous.

No, I'm not going! This is my vacation! They can call someone else. Fury keeps saying I have to be more than a friendly neighborhood Spider-Man, but . . . that's what I'm good at.

You're great at it!

Thanks, man. I just don't get why he's so pushy. There are so many adult hero people to handle this.

But, Peter, didn't you want to be treated as a grown-up?

And look where it got me!

. . . That's fair. Okay, whatever. You're awesome at being the friendly neighborhood Spider-Man, so that's what you'll be. And I'll always be your number one guy in the chair.

Very courtyard. Much big.

SUCH GOTH.

MUCH ANGST.

VERY WOW.

Such gold.

Please be better than this, you guys.

But we're not better than this, MJ. AND NEITHER ARE YOU! I saw you laughing. Don't pretend.

COOL STUFF WE SAW TODAY

(That were so touristy you may as
well have had an I ♡ NY shirt on.)

—A man painted silver, *doing the robot.*

> You could just go see that man in Times
> Square, Ned.

> But I'm a New Yorker. I never go to Times
> Square!

- Speaking of which, we saw a souvenir shop that
sold "authentic" New York souvenirs. I kind of wish
I'd bought a Statue of Liberty magnet for May.

> Wow, MJ. That was a really loud groan.
> How do I write that sound down?

GRRRoOoOOooOOO
ooAAAAANNNNnnN?

– Oh, and remember that American pizza place in Italy! That was a real wow—za moment for me. It was like I was home again.

I CAN'T BELIEVE YOU GUYS ATE AT A PLACE THAT SERVES "AMERICAN-STYLE" PIZZA WHILE WE'RE IN ITALY.

– What about that place we went to with the glassblowing? It was so cool.

MJ just put her head down on the table and is not going to talk to us for the rest of this meal, she says.

– Okay, but we *did* go to that bookstore, though.

Because you wanted to use the bathroom, Ned.

STILL COUNTS!

Maybe tomorrow we can go to Caffè Florian. At least to see it—it is waaaaay out of my budget.

Ned! MJ just got up and walked away.

GOOD! Now I can say that you should totally swing to the top of St. Mark's Basilica and get an awesome picture of me in the very middle of that square.

OMG.

Oh, and this SPIDEY-SENSE FAIL:

A pigeon pooped on me in St. Mark's Square.

We went to
CEMETERY ISLAND
and it was the COOLEST*

* *Scariest and quietest and* so many graves omg

So, the real name of this island is **Isola di San Michele**—and that just seems like <u>fate</u>. I was meant to go to this island. Apparently, Napoleon was like, **Venice! You have to bury your dead somewhere else, you can't just put them all over the city!** And Venice was like, **whoa, okay, relax, we have an island for that.**

And now you <u>know</u> that island is the **most** *haunted place on the planet.*

You have to admit, it was pretty beautiful. Did you see all the flowers? They were so pretty.

And all the grieving statues? So many gorgeous, sad little statues. Sad about their friends dying.

You are **both** so weird.

Maybe if two of us are weird and one of us isn't weird, then really the one person is the weirdo, and the two weird people are the not-weird people.

What?

I said what I said. Anyway, I wish we could stay on Cemetery Island.

Like overnight????

Can you imagine??

Nope, I don't want to imagine!
That sounds like having a waking nightmare, except I'm making my brain imagine a nightmare.

LOL, what if Betty came with us?

Well, obviously, that would change things, wouldn't it?

Today's Saddest Thing We Heard Mr. Harrington Say:

I used to have a car like that. But I bought it the day before the Battle of New York and my wife "died" in it.

A CATALOGING OF AMAZING T-SHIRTS MJ HAS WORN SINCE WE LEFT ON THIS TRIP:

- The one with Toni Morrison's face on it

- The one that quoted Eleanor Roosevelt: "No one can make you feel inferior without your consent."

- The one with Sojourner Truth's face on it

- The one that quoted Dolores Huerta: "Sí, se puede."

- The one with Marsha P. Johnson's face on it

- The one with the Rani of Jhansi's face on it

Peter, be creepier.

WHAT?

I think her shirts are cool. It's
not creepy to appreciate smart,
strong women on T-shirts...

Fiiiiiine,

pretend like you don't know
what I'm talking about.

...worn by smart, strong women.

THERE IT IS.

ITALIAN PIZZA VS. AMERICAN PIZZA

I'm team **ITALIAN PIZZA.** All the toppings were so fresh and so delicious. And we get our own pies. **Did I mention we each get our OWN PIES?** The fluffiest of fluffy crusts. And the one that just used olive oil instead of tomato sauce?

GENIUS.

Peter, you have been watching too many cooking TV shows.

Nah, it's about the palate, Ned. The palate.

You don't even know what a palate is!

It's ... important for food tasting!

AMERICAN PIZZA IS THE BEST, BECAUSE:

- SO MUCH CHEESE AND SAUCE

- And that super-thin crust.

- And also, you can get a whole slice for one single dollar. I didn't see a single one-Euro slice here, Pete.

- I don't know what it is, but there's something about the crust that's just so . . . homey. Like a warm cheesy blanket around my shoulders.

┌─────────────────────────────────┐
│ ITALIAN WOMEN WRITERS OF
│ HISTORY YOU SHOULD KNOW
└─────────────────────────────────┘

ITALIAN WOMEN WRITERS OF HISTORY YOU SHOULD KNOW

By MJ

I totally want to know more about women from history! Thanks for filling us in, MJ. ☺

This is really cool. Betty is going to think I'm so smart when I tell her about these kick-butt ladies tomorrow!

While giving MJ credit, of course.

Duh!

Here's a thing you should know about Italy . . . there have been outspoken feminists there since, like, the 1300s. That is hundreds and hundreds of years before America was even a dream in a colonizer's eyes!

LUCREZIA MARINELLA

She was a writer during the Renaissance and published over decades. Can you even imagine? It's 1600 and you're a noblewoman and you

86

decide you're going to write books and your family is like, "Yes, dear Lucrezia, yes." And then you write <u>books</u>. Pro-woman books!

MODERATA FONTE

My girl Fonte was a child prodigy, orphaned by the plague, and wrote a book called *The Worth of Women*, which is one of the earliest known works to deal with roles of the genders. I love her. She married pretty late for the times, <u>and</u> her husband signed over the full control of her finances to her. In 1500s Italy.

CHRISTINE DE PIZAN

Christine de Pizan (born in Venice!) wrote a book called *The Book of the City of Ladies* in the 1400s. <u>Fourteen hundreds</u>. Basically, some dude was like "Well, women aren't really worth anything." And Christine was like, "Oh, no. Let me tell you exactly why women are important and amazing, and I'm going to use all these cool women from history to do it." Owned.

— PHOTO OPS —
RECOMMENDED BY SPIDER-MAN

(as told to Ned because Spidey and I
are <u>very</u> close friends)

1. The dome inside of St. Mark's Basilica: Crawl
   inside the dome and you can get the most epic
   selfie of you and at least seven or eight saints.

2. Swing across the Grand Canal for a unique shot
   of the Ponte di Rialto straight on.*
   > * You may fall into the Grand Canal
   >   again. Or for the first time. Because as
   >   Spider-Man, you are far too athletic
   >   to fall into the Grand Canal.

3. St. Mark's Campanile
The top of this tower has a huge gold angel
Gabriel at the top and it is <u>so cool</u>. And if
you get the right angle, it looks like you're
photobombing him!

4. IN A GONDOLA.

NED: Wait, this is just a normal photo.

SPIDEY: Yeah, but it looks hilarious to see
Spider-Man hanging out in a gondola lol

NED: True.

VENICE:
HIGHS AND LOWS!

HIGH: Taking a gondola ride with my bae, and cementing our power couple status with the best ship-name, ever: Netty. OR, equal high: Nick Fury shot me with a tranquilizer dart, omg.

LOW: Going to Cemetery Island with MJ.

HIGH: Going to Cemetery Island with MJ! (Really, Ned, it wasn't so bad.)

You're only saying that because you like MJ.

I thought it was interesting!

You think MJ is interesting.

Because she is!

LOW: ... Finding a certain former **S.H.I.E.L.D.** director waiting for me in a dark hotel room like a super creep. Or was it falling into the Grand Canal? Maybe it was when I was bad at my other job and someone named Mysterio did it better than I could.

BACKPACKS LOST SINCE WE LEFT NEW YORK

1 - when web-head had to team-up with Mr. Mysterious Man

1 - when I was getting that selfie at the top of the basilica

1 - when we went for gelato and a tourist fell in the Grand Canal and Spider-Man had to save them

TOTAL: 3

VENICE MEMORIES

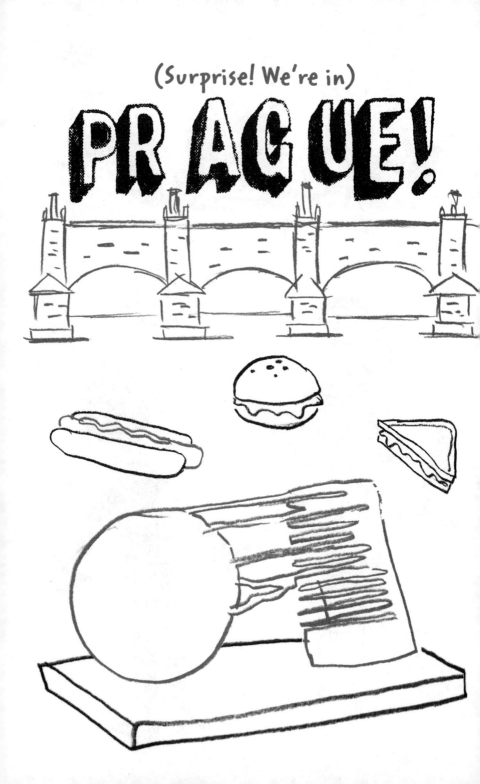

I can't believe we have to go to Prague because someone bogarted our trip.

I CAN'T BELIEVE WE GET TO GO TO PRAGUE ON AN ADVENTURE.

I also have a new suit.

WAIT, WHAT??

YEAH. New suit. Kind of excited to test it out!

WHAT IS IT LIKE?!

I don't know yet! It's cool? Yeah. It's cool!

You have to take it out for a spin, Peter. You have to.

Okay, okay. BRB.

NEW SUIT PROS AND CONS

PROS:

- The stealthiest suit ever. No one will ever see me coming! (Take that, evildoers, SPIDEY STEALTH ATTACK!)

- Everyone looks cooler in black, and honestly, I feel like a grown-up New Yorker.

- The epic flip-up lenses.

- The fingerless gloves are very It's-Called-Fashion-Look-It-Up.

- I think the stealth is so important that it actually gets two points on a PROS list. Stealth!

CONS:

- Really there's just one con to this suit.

What is it?

- Well, I got a wedgie. The wedgie was bad. The suit gives bad wedgies.

97

Prague has the second ugliest building in the world, Ned.

What do you think the ugliest building in the world is?

There's a joke here about Flash's personality, but I'm honestly too tired to think of it.

Why so tired, Parker?

Just, uh, you know. Um. I didn't get a chance to sleep much last night? I was really looking forward to Paris, that's it. I know you wanted to see those skull tunnels. Right?

NICE SAVE, PETE!

I did. But I think Prague will scratch that itch. It's got some really cool, weird stuff.

What does that mean???

Oh, you'll see, Ned.
YOOOOOU'LL SEE.

WHO IS BETTER AT MAKING OUR LIVES HARD?

BRAD DAVIS

- Has annoyingly perfect hair and got to sit next to MJ on the plane <u>and</u> on the bus.

- Tried to tell MJ I'm dating random girls in Europe????

- Walked in on me changing. Rude.

FLASH THOMPSON

– Jerk with a big head who calls his internet fans the FLASHMOB.

I can't believe we found someone worse than Flash Thompson. What is this world??

TOP THINGS TO DO IN PRAGUE

(based on even <u>less</u> internet research than Venice)

(Because we *didn't know* we were coming!)

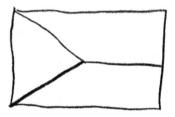

"Prague is the city of cobblestones and history and love."

—A very weird travel site we found.

Wow, cobblestones.

WALK ACROSS THE CHARLES BRIDGE

This is supposed to have **incredible views** during the day and night, so I'm going to go twice.

Oh yeah, I wanted to get some pictures for May, so I'll come with you.

Pictures for May, uh–huh.

OLD TOWN SQUARE

You know this one is actually shaped like a square?

Why _isn't_ Times Square shaped like a square?

THE PRAGUE
ASTRONOMICAL CLOCK

This is in the Old Town Square and the internet said that if you get there at the right time it has all these clockwork models that do a dance or something.

And if you pay five bucks, you can get to the top for a spectacular view.

I have other ideas about getting a spectacular view.

NED.

EXPLORE PRAGUE CASTLE

So many castles! Who knew I liked castles so much?

Maybe you were supposed to be, like, a king's advisor in your last life.

You'd be a knight, for sure.

This would make a great movie, omg.

You are so right.

. . . You know we'd all die in like five seconds if we went back in time because of how diseased and dirty it was, right?

But then we could come back as really cool ghosts.

WALLENSTEIN GARDEN

There are white peacocks in this garden. Do you think Betty would want a peacock as a gift?

You . . . can't take a peacock, Ned.

They're not that big, are they?

MALÁ STRANA

Everything in Prague is so _old_.

Not every country can be a baby country.

Lol imagine a baby country peeing in a diaper.

Lol.

MJ'S ITINERARY FOR PRAGUE

★ PRAGUE OLD TOWN GHOSTS ★
AND MYSTERIES TOUR

Can you imagine if we got to see a ghost?

NO THANK YOU.

★ NIGHTTIME ALCHEMY AND ★
DARK SCIENCE TOUR

MJ, how do you find these?

I searched for "weird gothic tours Prague" on my phone.

... The description says we're going to go through a lot of dark alleys. That sounds ...

Like work?

Scary. It sounds scary.

★ MUSEUM OF MEDIEVAL ★
TORTURE INSTRUMENTS

MJ, NO!

MJ, YES!

★ MAKE A MARIONETTE ★

Is that one of those creepy wooden puppets?

Do you mean, is that one of those incredible models of Czech culture and tradition?

Yes.

Then, yes.

★ SEE THE UPSIDE-DOWN STATUE ★

Okay, now _that_ sounds cool.

Yeah! It's a statue of a dude riding an upside-down horse.

Wait. What? How?

You'll have to wait and see!

★ MUSEUM OF COMMUNISM ★

MJ, this sounds like homework.

I think it's fascinating.

It is, I'm very interested in communism, MJ. I'll come with you.

Thanks, Peter.

TO: science-euro-trip distribution group
FROM: MR. DELL
Subject: UPDATED ITINERARY

Dear Students,

Please see the attached updated itinerary to include our impromptu detour to Prague. I did some last-minute research and found relevant sites for us to see. I'm sorry to miss our stops in Paris, but Prague has some excellent science-based opportunities for your assignment.

Mr. Dell

Attachment UPDATED SCIENCE TRIP.DOC

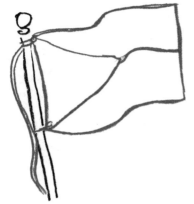

Mr. Dell's Updated Science Itinerary

PRAGUE

National Technical Museum

Actually, Pete, this is probably a good one for you to go to.

WHY IS THAT, NEDANIEL?

You think Ned is short for <u>Nedaniel</u>?

Don't try to distract me, Petrova.

YOU THINK PETER IS SHORT FOR PETROVA???

Nighttime Alchemy and Dark Science Tour

Look, I told you!

Yeah, you and Mr. Dell have the same taste.

The same <u>great</u> taste.

Tesla Monument

TESLA FTW

YEAH TESLA

TESLAAAA! EDISON WAS A HACK!

Wow, we really are all nerds.

Listen, in our house we respect Nikola Tesla as a true genius.

SPIDER-MAN'S RULES FOR SWINGING THROUGH EUROPE

(as told to Ned because Spidey and I are friends, obviously)

1. Do not use historical landmarks to tether. Europeans are not okay with web–fluid stuck to their precious arcs.

2. Find cushionier suit shoes for landing on cobblestones.* *Ouch. My feet.

3. Remember that Venice is the one with all the water and aim your trajectory accordingly.

4. Pigeons in Europe are older and more vicious than New York pigeons; don't forget this. Not saying these pigeons are evil, but we're not NOT saying that, either.

5. Do NOT use the Prague Astronomical Clock to swing at any time on the hour because your webbing WILL get pulled into the gears and a lot of people will see you get very stuck and it will be very embarrassing.

CZECH PHRASES WE MIGHT WANT TO LEARN

(translated by an internet translator)

English: I don't speak Czech.
Czech: Nemluvím česky.

English: I have to go to the bathroom.
Czech: Musím jít do koupelny.

English: How much is this?
Czech: Kolik to je?

English: I'm lost.
Czech: Ztratil jsem se.

English: Help me!
Czech: Pomoz mi!

English: That person took my purse!
Czech: Ten osoba mi vzal kabelku!

English: Where is the man with eight legs?
Czech: Kde je ten muž s osmi nohama?

These are . . . weirdly specific, you guys.
You never know what you'll need to know!

English: Spider-Man.
Czech: Pavoučí Muž.

SOME <u>INCREDIBLE</u> <u>CZECH WOMEN</u> WE SHOULD ALL KNOW

I love these, MJ! I feel like I'm becoming a better feminist!

Yeah, I can't wait to CZECH these out!

NBJ FTW!

Betty was really impressed with the Italian women, so thanks for keeping these coming, MJ! She also said that you're a good influence on me (but she doesn't know that we're good influences on you, too! I saw you laugh at my NBJ lol).

This was a surprise stop, so I had to do some research on the fly . . . and Prague and the surrounding countries have such a complicated history, it was kind of hard. But I found some really, really amazing women!

FRANTIŠKA PLAMÍNKOVÁ

Františka, or Frannie, as we'll call her because I like to think we'd be friends, helped get Czech women the right to vote. She was the ultimate suffragette. When she found out that there wasn't a law against women running for local, low-level elections, she got some ladies to run! Those races became a snowball that turned into a national symbol for women.

ALICE MASARYKOVÁ

Alice was a woman of the people. She really believed in democracy and making sure that everyone felt represented. Alice is also one of the founders of social education in Czechoslovakia... meaning, she helped people learn how to help people.

THINGS MR. HARRINGTON THINKS ARE COOL BUT ARE THE WORST

THE OPERA

WE HAVE TO PUT ON TIES AND GO TO THE OPERA

And Mr. Dell said I couldn't wear my hat. Did you know we couldn't wear hats to the opera???

Okay, Peter, but counterpoint.

Ned, you're answering your own point. You're counterpointing yourself.

Keep up, *buddy*. At the opera, we can totally sit next to Betty and MJ.

...Go on.

We can share opera glasses. And then we'll have to sit close together. And *SNUGGLE*.

Snuggling is good. Snuggling sounds good. Right? I don't know if I can snuggle with MJ. Is there another word for snuggle so I can just ...ask her without sounding like a dweeb?

Pretty Eventful First Day in Prague
UNDERSTATEMENT OF THE YEAR

A brief example of what (probably) went through web-head's, uh, head for the entire fire elemental fight.

OH MY GOSH THAT FIRE THING IS SO BIG OH NO OH NO OH NO IT'S BURNING MY WEB-FLUID WHERE IS MYSTERIO OH THERE HE IS OH THANK GOODNESS BECAUSE I AM VERY SCARED BUT AT LEAST—OH NO THERE HE GOES, SWATTED DOWN BY THE FIRE MONSTER FROM THOSE SHORT-PEOPLE-GO-ON-AN-ADVENTURE MOVIES HOW DO I FIX THIS OKAY OKAY PETER GET IT TOGETHER YOU'RE SPIDER-MAN YOU CAN DO THIS

Wow, Ned, that seems really, really accurate. Can you read minds????

Peter, you wrote this and handed me a note to put it in the journal.

HOW ARE YOU SO BAD AT SECRETS?

ANYWAY, the opera was pretty decent minus having to leave early and all that!

Oh yeah? Who knew the opera could be fun?

Where'd you disappear to after all the action died down anyway?

Nowhere special...
EXCEPT THAT MYSTERIO TOOK ME OUT TO TALK.

WHAAAAAAT

He helped me figure out some web-head stuff, it was good talking to someone who gets it.

Would you say that he became a little less mysterious? #NBJ Oh, speaking of which, MJ was looking for you. She ran after you when you left the opera.

WHAT??

SPIDER-MAN, SPIDER-MAN

Should we really be that blatant? I'm a little worried that someone is going to see all this secret stuff. . . .

We're safe! We've been doing it all trip *and* no one has figured it out.

It's only a matter of time!

Dude. We know what we're doing.

Sometimes. Sometimes we know what we're doing. . . . Ned, I can feel you glaring at me. Quit it.

Oh, is that MJ coming? Should we show her?

NED!

How Ned imagines the scene of Peter on the Charles Bridge at sunrise with MJ

Starring: Peter Parker and Michelle "MJ" Jones

EXT. CHARLES BRIDGE, SUNRISE
THE WEATHER IS BEAUTIFUL
THE SKY IS PINK AND ORANGE
LIGHTS ARE GLEAMING ON THE WATER.

OUR HERO, PETER PARKER [MALE, 16,
PRETTY GOOD-LOOKING I GUESS BUT LOOKS
LIKE HE HASN'T SLEPT IN THREE DAYS]

Well, I haven't!

You should do our skin care routine, it'll help even when you don't get sleep.

...Aren't you supposed to be writing a script or something?

Oh, yeah!

STANDS NEXT TO MICHELLE "MJ" JONES,
LEANING OVER THE BRIDGE'S RAILING.
THEY'RE ALONE. IT'S VERY ROMANTIC.

Ned, omg, you're killing me.

Please don't interrupt my creative genius,
thank you.

MJ
So, that's a beautiful sunrise, isn't it?

PETER FALLS OFF THE BRIDGE.

That did not happen!

Okay, okay, let me try again.

MJ
So, that's a beautiful sunrise, isn't it?

PETER
Je ne parle pas anglais. Mais oui!
Le fromage! La table!

That for sure did not happen, buddy. Also, we're in Prague. Why am I speaking French here? I wouldn't yell at MJ about cheese and tables, by the way.

Look, I only took French 1 and not Czech 1. Stop focusing on the details!

MJ
So, that's a beautiful sunrise, isn't it?

PETER
MJ, you are so beautiful in the morning light.
I love you. Let's date!

NED!!!

MJ
So, that's a beautiful sunrise, isn't it?

PETER IS DISTRACTED BY MJ'S BEAUTY.

PETER
Huh? Yeah, definitely. Anyway, check out that sunrise!

PETER'S VOICE GETS HIGHER AND HIGHER AS
HE TRIES TO ACTUALLY CONVERSE WITH MJ.

Not even a little bit true.
Okay, maybe a little.

Today's Saddest Thing We Heard
Mr. Harrington Say:

Oh, Prague has some
of the oldest standing
monuments in the world. I
should ask if they'll build
one for my marriage.

#yikes

BEST PRAGUE STREET FOODS FOR SWINGING

1. TRDELNÍK

It's basically a grilled doughnut, shaped like a cylinder, and filled with whatever you want. Ice cream? Do it. Grilled walnuts? Hazelnuts? Yes, please. Topped with powdered sugar? Energy for days! Prague is really bringing its "you can hold the delicious food in one hand" game.

2. GRILOVANÉ KLOBÁSY

This Prague version of grabbing a hot dog on a busy corner in New York City made me feel right at home. A sausage in a roll with just a touch of mustard? Delicioso! I mean, lahodný!

3. PRAGUE HAM

So salty and mouthwateringly good. It will get your suit gloves a little greasy, but it's a small price to pay for how tasty this food is. I'll take greasy fingertips any day. Yes, it was worth slipping down the side of that building, Ned.

4. FRIED CHEESE SANDWICH

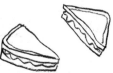

An actual fried piece of cheese in between two buns might not sound good on paper, but ooh boy. Put this bad boy in your pocket, hop over to the bell tower, and relax with some cheesy goodness.

5. LANGOŠE

This may be an acquired taste. A round, flat disk of fried dough, covered in ketchup and . . . you guessed it, cheese. It's almost pizza-esque, which is why I'd recommend it. But it's not pizza. So you'd be widening your horizons by eating it. I think.

Mr. Dell really loves his scientist facts. What did he say again? Leo made some Czechs cry?

He said, "It's not a far cry from Leonardo da Vinci's work to the work of these Czech scientists and engineers."

Oh. Same same.

Can you believe that display of all the old cell phones? They were so big. How did they even fit into people's pockets??

I think they used to clip them to their belts.

That is Big Yikes. Oh man, I never would've been able to keep a cell phone in my suit. Aunt May would never let me be Spider-Man in the past!

You should make a spider-mobile.

What?

I dunno, all those cool cars got me thinking that when you get your driver's license you should totally get a spider-buggy or something.

GrROOooOOOAANnnnn

Whoa, you and MJ have been hanging out a lot, huh, Pete?

SPIDEY SENSE FAILS:

MJ walked up behind Peter while he was totally and 100,000,000 percent picking a wedgie out of his butt.

Dude!! Why???

WORDS NED IS NO
LONGER ALLOWED TO SAY:

BAE

But how else am I supposed to refer to my Before Anyone Else???

NOT MY PROBLEM, BUD.

HONEY

Okay, but if I just want, I don't know, honey for a biscuit or something?

Call it Bee-Juice.

Ewwwww.

LOVELY

PETER, YOU ARE BEING RIDICULOUS

NETTY

NOOOOOOOO

BETTY

I have to be allowed to say my girlfriend's <u>name</u>!

Should have thought of that before you over-used it, okay?

This is revenge for the spidey-sense fail, huh?

Maybe.

♥ NED'S ♥ ROMANCE REC

Running out of things to talk about?
Write her an acrostic poem!

BEAUTIFUL

ETHEREAL

TOTALLY COOL

TIMELY   Timely?
Yeah, like, she's always perfectly on time.

I don't think that's what "timely" means.

YOU'RE REALLY SMART

I feel like this acrostic is
getting away from you.

BOSS

RADIANT

ADORABLE

NICE

TENDER
   Way to bring it
   back at the end!

Today's Saddest Thing We Heard
Mr. Harrington Say:

I don't think
Edison was that
bad, was he?

TESLA vs. EDISON

A conversation between MJ and Mr. Harrington

MJ: Mr. Harrington, we cannot possibly celebrate a man who was so money-hungry that he cut down all his competition and kept us from having a chance at clean energy decades earlier.

Mr. Harrington: He couldn't have been ... that ... bad?

MJ: He experimented on elephants.

Mr. Harrington: Okay, okay, Tesla is our guy.

NED'S IDEAS FOR SPIDEY PHOTO OPS

Or, places you can swing me to get great photos*
*As long as they're not too dangerous

1. The top of Prague Castle: It won't be too dangerous because there are turrets. I want to take photos in front of the turrets.

2. The upside-down statue: We can take a picture of us sitting behind the king on a dead horse.

3. The top of the Old Town Bridge Tower: Again, not dangerous because you've already been there.

4. Henry's Bell Tower: We can RING THE BELL, Peter!

5. The Dancing House: I'll web up a camera across the way to get us at the top. It'll look really cool, I promise.

Does the building move?

What? No.

Well, you said it was _dancing!_

I'm gonna tag that one as #NBJ.

PRAGUE

HIGHS AND LOWS!

HIGH: Fighting a fire elemental and **LIVING TO TELL THE TALE.** Lastly, eating grilled dough filled with hazelnut stuffing.

LOW: Uh ... having to fight a big fire monster.

Ooooh, grilled dough. Excellent choice.
Okay, my turn!

HIGH: Riding a Ferris wheel with Betty.

LOW: I think I have to agree with you and say the fire dude. Although . . . it did lead to my high, so I'm changing my answer to having to wear a tie to the opera.

MORE BACKPACKS LOST SINCE WE LEFT NEW YORK

1 - I left in the tower when I was keeping watch for the fire elemental

1 - I just forgot in our hotel room. Oops.

1 - I dropped while swinging and holding on to my trdelnik at the same time

1 - webbed up to the inside of a bell at Henry's Bell Tower and I couldn't get it out because the bell started ringing

TOTAL BACKPACKS LOST ON TRIP: 7

TOP THINGS TO DO IN BERLIN

I'm sure Berlin is great, but I got to see even less than I saw last time, which is saying something because last time I basically only saw an airport.

Oh wait, I did get to eat Bretzen! It's a very soft pretzel with salt, and I can hold it while being judged by three very strict, scary adults. Though they might tell you to put it down and will frown if you don't listen and instead shove the whole thing in your mouth.

Then the fourth adult will give you a sad look because you didn't offer him any before you scarfed it down.

Lastly, do not recommend shoving a whole Bretzen in your mouth and trying to eat it because you'll probably choke a little bit and fall over trying to get to a water bottle.

I'll say it for Ned, since he's not here:
THAT OLE PARKER LUCK STRIKES AGAIN.

A LIST OF SCARY PEOPLE WHO WORK FOR NICK FURY AND HOW CINNAMON ROLL-Y THEY ARE

MARIA HILL:
looks like a cinnamon roll but could actually hurt you

DIMITRI:
looks like he could hurt you and could actually hurt you; there is no cinnamon roll in Dimitri

QUENTIN BECK:
looks like a cinnamon roll; is a cinnamon roll (I think)

This journal is a lot less fun without my friends writing in it, too.

141

In honor of MJ:

GERMAN <u>WOMEN</u> OF HISTORY YOU <u>SHOULD KNOW!</u>

HILDEGARD OF BINGEN

According to the internet: Hildegard of Bingen (I need to change my name to Spider-Man of Forest Hills, like, immediately. It sounds so much more intimidating.) Where was I? Oh, right! According to the internet: Hildegard was an octo-threat. She was a leader, a mystic, a musician, a writer, a philosopher, a scientist, an abbess, and a linguist. And this was all in the one thousands! As in, 1000 C.E.

UGH, the grown-ups are calling in to my suit.
Guess it's time to go!

<u>More Backpacks Lost Since We Left New York</u>

1 - I left in the secret Fury lair oops

TOTAL BACKPACKS LOST ON TRIP: 8

BERLIN MEMORIES:

Well, that was interesting.

Do you mean how it looked like you and MJ were talking _a lot_?

PETER & MJ'S COUPLE NAME OPTIONS!

PeeJay:

No! Ned. NO! MJ and I do _not_ need a couple name.

MJete:

Really, we don't need a couple name, Ned.

NED!!

Sorry, just reacting to the fact that you're turning bright red right now even _talking_ about it.

OMG.

ANYWAY, I'm excited to have some time to just hang out in London for a day or two before we have to get back. Fury's gonna deal with the fallout so I can finally actually have a relaxing vacation with my best buds.

Careful, Peter, famous last words, et cetera.

Oh no, I need to find some wood to knock on!

I still can't believe that we got saved by Nicholas Fury. Nick Fury talked to me. Nick Fury <u>might know my name</u>.

He definitely knows your name, Ned. Trust me. He probably knows your school ID number.

Shut up.

MJ would probably say it's the government infringing on our right to privacy.

Lol she totally would, but I meant shut up as in *THAT IS SO COOL.*

PETER'S ROMANCE REC:

Don't make up a couple name.*
*I can't condone this statement.

TOP THINGS TO DO IN LONDON

(Because we have time! Yeah!)

(I can't believe we got to go to extra
cities during this trip!)

PICCADILLY CIRCUS

I really hate to be the bearer of bad news but . . .
I feel like I have a moral responsibility to tell you
that Piccadilly Circus is not actually a circus.

Ughhh, well, that one is crossed
off the list.

Yeah, it's sort of like Times Square.

Ugh, capital N-capital-T-No-Thanks.

STONEHENGE

Oh buddy, I have more bad news for you. Stonehenge isn't in London.

HOW ARE WE GOING TO BECOME WIZARDS IF WE CAN'T EVEN GET TO STONEHENGE, PETE.

There are people we can ask about that, I feel like.

BOROUGH MARKET

You want to go to a grocery store?

No, no, it is this huge outdoor market that has so many different kinds of food.

Oh, heck yes. One of those places where I can get, like, paella and a turnover within three minutes of each other?

YES!!!!

You both have a one-track mind.

Oh, do you not want to go and check out the Plague Pasties stall?

...I think I want to go to that.

TOWER OF LONDON

Should we try to actually see this without getting almost blown up by a giant monster?

I think the crown jewels are there!

Ehhh, I don't really want to pay to see a bunch of big, shiny rocks.

That's a fair point; let's skip it.

GLOBE THEATRE

Oh, yeah! Let's go to this one.

Like, see a Shakespeare play?

Wait, what? I thought it was a theater shaped like a sphere?

It is, but they do Shakespeare in it, I think.

Did you guys pay <u>any</u> attention in English class???

AFTERNOON TEA

This one we are *definitely doing*. It is an hour and a half of a million tiny sandwiches.

I'm sold. Let's do it.

Okay, yeah, I want in on this, too.

BRITISH VOCABULARY LESSONS

Sometimes words can mean very different things in England, so a quick lesson:

American: Trash can

British: Bin

American: Apartment

British: Flat

American: French fries

British: Chips

This seems needlessly confusing.

American: Potato chips

British: Crisps

Seriously, needlessly confusing!

American: Cookie

British: Biscuit

Now I just think the British are trolling us.

American: Jell-O

British: Jelly

Ew, that is <u>not</u> a mistake I want to make.

THIS ONE IS VERY IMPORTANT:

American: Pants

British: UNDERWEAR

Okay, now I just think we're destined for as many awkward experiences as humanly possible.

Saddest thing we heard Mr. Harrington say today:

Wow, that was such a familiar adventure that I almost feel like someone else must have faked their death. Hashtag memories!

MJ'S ITINERARY FOR LONDON

History of the Plague Walking Tour

MJ, WHY.

London has maybe the most famous known history of the plague. It was everywhere and no one was safe!!

Did it just get colder in here?

Jack the Ripper Walking Tour

Jack the Ripper like...?

Yup! I think they do this one at night.

MJ, you are <u>very</u> scary.

Which is great, because then she can keep us safe when we go on this horrifying walking tour.

Black Heritage at the Victoria and Albert Museum

Ooh this sounds awesome, I am definitely coming to this with you.

I'd expect no less ☺

African and Caribbean War Memorial

And this!

YEAH! They just unveiled it a few years ago, but it's supposed to be really incredible.

The parking lot where they found Richard III's remains

This one isn't in London, so to speak, but let's take a day trip to find it.

We can take a day trip to see this, but not Stonehenge???

I have a feeling that neither one of these things are going to work out.

Clowns Gallery-Museum

MJ, no!

MJ, YES!

MJ, why.

MJ says because it's going to be creepy and great.

The Viktor Wynd Museum of Curiosities, Fine Art, and Natural History

Oh, this sounds nice and safe.

If you like taxidermy and weird skeletons, it is totally safe.

PETER'S LIST OF CUTEST
UNDERGROUND STATION NAMES

1. PADDINGTON STATION

I wish every station was named after a
cuddly bear.

2. BARKING STATION

Obviously, this has to be listed because it
reminds me of puppies and puppies are cute.

3. ELEPHANT AND CASTLE STATION

Okay, I realize that I'm picking a lot of animal-
sounding stations. But an elephant in a castle?
Can you imagine??

4. PICCADILLY CIRCUS STATION

I know it's not a circus but it still **SOUNDS
LIKE ONE.**

5. CHARING CROSS STATION

I don't know why I like this one, maybe I just like how it sounds in a British accent:

CHAH-ring Crohss.

SPIDEY-SENSE FAIL:

A kick to the door locked Peter in the public toilet and he never saw it coming.

I'm regretting telling you about spidey-sense.

PETER AND NED'S RULES OF ETIQUETTE

We've been in London for enough time to figure out exactly how Etiquettish one must be to be considered Proper.

"Etiquettish" is not a word.

Sure it is!
Call us the Etiquettish Masters, please.

• One must always refer to oneself as "one" because "one" is much more regal than the lowly "I," wouldn't you say, Petrova?

Oh yes, Nedaniel. "One" is far more polite and regal than "I."

- One must also remember to keep one pinkie finger stuck completely out when holding <u>anything</u>. A teacup, a fork, a plate, a pizza, a book, a basketball, honestly every single thing that exists that can be held. No pinkie should ever touch it.

- When attending a party, one should always bring a gift. Preferably handmade. A drawing, perhaps. Or a nice pot holder.

- If one finds oneself at dinner with a friend, remember to always let the friend take off their hat first. Never take one's own hat off first. It's considered <u>very</u> gauche.

Do you even know what "gauche" means???

...I assume it's related to guacamole somehow. Like, you're green. Like an avocado. And hard on the inside. Instead of soft and squishy. Soft and squishy is good. Hard on the inside is bad.

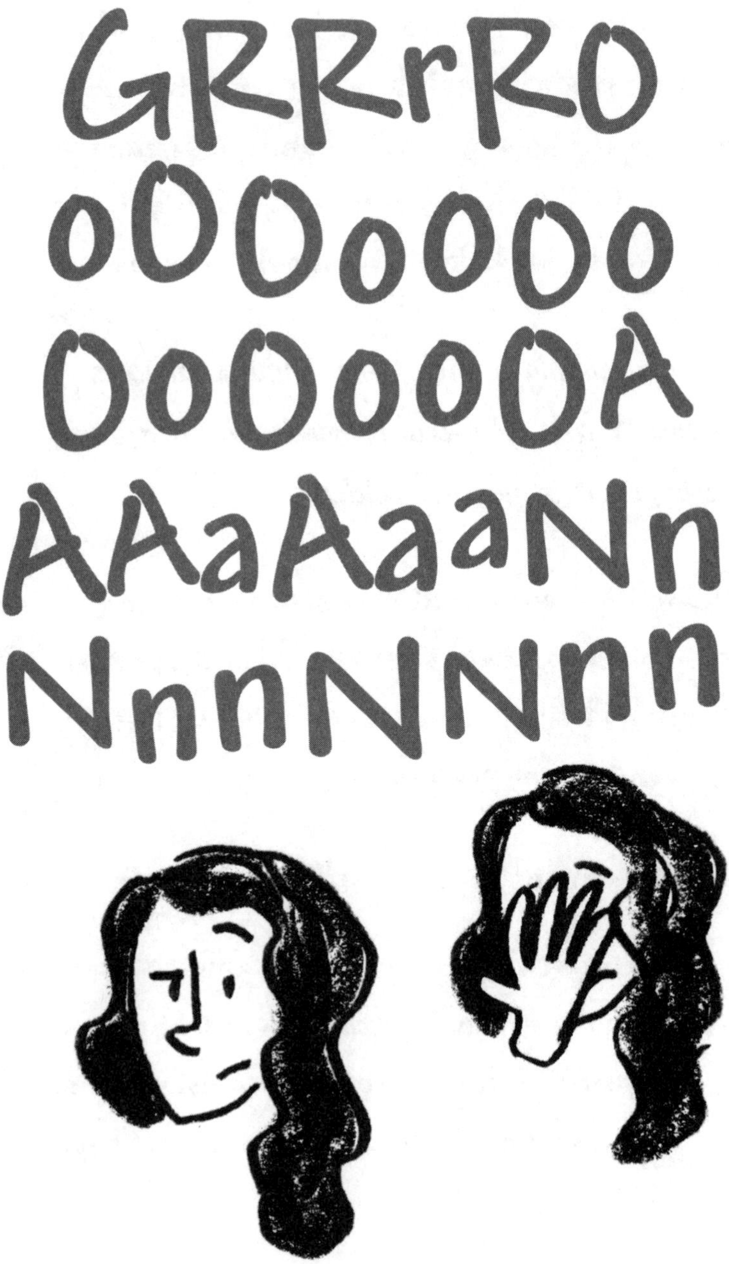
GRRrRO
oOOoOOo
OoOooOA
AAaAaaNn
NnnNNnn

• When groaning at one's friends, one should really cover one's mouth.

Yes, to not cover one's mouth is very gauche.

• And as one knows, to be "gauche" is very bad.

You are both the worst.

Does this count as a **NBJ**?

BEST FOODS IN ENGLAND FOR SWINGING AROUND

1. A PASTY!

This is a delicious tiny pie filled with various delicious things. You can eat it one-handed, leaving you free to swing from building to building! And if you need both hands, it's small enough to hold in your mouth!

2. Scotch Egg

This is a boiled egg wrapped in meat and then deep-fried. All of those things sound good by themselves, and when you put them together? It's a holy trinity of perfection sitting in your belly. And you can keep a few in a web-backpack for easy access! They're so little!

3. Potato Skins

I can't say no to a potato skin that has things in it. Like. They're little boats. Little potato boats for my mouth.

4. Toastie

A toastie is the English version of a grilled cheese sandwich. A. Grilled. Cheese. Sandwich. I can eat like five grilled cheese sandwiches in a row. Spider-metabolism!

5. Tandoori Chicken

Okay, this one is great but also dangerous. It's spicy, bright orange chicken on the bone that you can totally eat on the go . . . but it is so spicy. Your mouth might light on fire, and maybe you'll accidentally-on-purpose fall into the River Thames for a reprieve from the burning. But really, then you can take a second bite.

We've been in several separate countries now, and I think it's time to take a look back at some of MY favorite That Ole Parker Luck moments across Europe!

Ned, NOOOOOOO.

WE MUST, PETE, FOR THE INTEGRITY OF THE JOURNAL!

– Not being able to wash your spidey-suit, so that old lady called you "L'Uomo Rancido"

– Or when you jumped into a moving car because you thought it was being stolen, but really it was just a girl who was learning how to drive, and then she screamed and you screamed and it ended really poorly?

. . . There was that time that an evil pigeon distracted me and I mashed a kebab into my mask in Prague.

That's the spirit!

- And there was that time that I got to talk to MJ on the bridge.

I don't know if that counts as Ole Parker Luck. . . .

True, it was definitely **IN SPITE** of my Ole Parker Luck and not because of it.

Okay, you're gross and ruined this part of the journal.

BEST SPIDEY PHOTO OPS IN LONDON!

1. TOP OF ST. PAUL'S CATHEDRAL

Luckily, having web-shooters means that you don't have to climb eight million stairs to get to the top of St. Paul's for an incredible view. Your friends might be a little miffed that you won't swing them up to the top because there were always too many people around, though.

2. THE LONDON EYE

Okay, so technically you don't <u>need</u> to be Spidey to get this shot, unless you want to be on the outside of the Ferris wheel carriage. Which I do. Because it's way cooler than the inside of the Ferris wheel carriage.

3. THE GHERKIN!

No, this isn't a tiny pickle even though it sounds like it and it is sort of the shape of one? Or maybe a 1950s rocket ship? It has a very cool spiral pattern, and the very tip-top looks like a beautiful flower. Probably a good spot for a photo for two people.

I'll totally come with you, Pete!

... Ned, I might have meant someone else.

4. THE GLOBE THEATRE

Okay, for this one, wait until two in the morning, and web up the open circle at the top of the Globe Theatre. Lie back, and take in the view of that night sky. Sure, you could do this at the top of any flat building, but there's something nice about being able to fall back onto a web. It's just different than concrete and metal!

5. BUCKINGHAM PALACE

What makes this cool is sticking to the side of the palace, and trying to get a selfie that has the whole front facade from a really cool angle.

Wait, OR, hear me out. You know how those guards aren't supposed to react to anything and people try to get them to break???? What if you crouched on top of one of their hats and I can take your picture.

I think that would kick off an international incident and I would get in a <u>lot</u> of trouble.

But wouldn't it be worth it for the Insta post??

NO!

You're not gonna say Big Ben?

It felt too touristy?

I can hear MJ applauding from here! Although the rest of the list still feels pretty touristy.

Well, then...

6. BIG BEN

Now it feels like MJ is giving us both the evil eye!

AND NOW, another award-winning script from Nedaniel!

Despite that disaster etiquette lesson from earlier, I really appreciate you leaning into Nedaniel, Nedaniel.

Anything for your joy, MJ. But let's script the conversation between MJ and the guide at the Tower of London.

Wait, what?

WELCOME TO THE JOURNAL, MJ!

EXT. TOWER OF LONDON

IT'S A GRAY DAY. A STORM IS ON THE HORIZON, AND WE DON'T JUST MEAN THE WEATHER.

I'm going to stop you right there, Ned. I think <u>I'll</u> write a script about the conversation that you had with Betty before you all went into the tower.

Oh, look. All of a sudden my script is for a <u>very</u> short short film.

> TOWER OF LONDON GUIDE
> Hello, miss!

> MJ
> No, thank you.

THE END

That's what I thought.

BRITISH WOMEN OF HISTORY YOU SHOULD KNOW

1. SOPHIA DULEEP SINGH

Sophia was the daughter of an exiled Sikh king, which makes her an In Real Life princess. That makes her exciting, but since she was born into it and didn't make active choices to get there, it's not why she's on this list. The reason she's on this list is that she was a leading member of the cause for women's right to vote. She used her title to bring attention to her causes and that makes her a rock star.

2. PHILLIS WHEATLEY

Phillis Wheatley spent part of her life as an enslaved person in the American colonies, but was freed after she moved to England and went on to become the first published Black poet in 1773. Seventeen Seventy-Three!!

3. MARY SEACOLE

I'm sure you've heard of Florence Nightingale, but she wasn't the only selfless British nurse. Mary Seacole was a Black woman who applied to help during the Crimean War effort in the mid-1800s, but they wouldn't let her. So, you know what Ms. Seacole did? She went on her own! She opened a "British Hotel" that would exist to take care of British soldiers. No one could tell her no!

COOL STUFF WE SAW TODAY

(These are a <u>tiny</u> bit less touristy than the last round. I'm very proud of you guys.)

A very cool band busking in Trafalgar Square. One of them was using an actual washboard to make music. **A washboard!**

> I had no idea you could even
> make music with a washboard.

> Yeah, this was definitely one of the
> coolest things we've seen the whole trip.

Wax royals! They look so real!

> Yeah, I can't believe you said
> "excuse me" to a wax princess.
> ## LOL.

I'm a polite boy, don't hate.

I take the "proud" comment back.

We went to the London Dungeon because we thought you'd like it, MJ.

It was pretty decent, but it was like
the kiddie-park version of a dungeon.
Now, the torture museum, that's the stuff.

I'm trying to forget we went to that, OMG.

LONDON:
— HIGHS AND LOWS! —

HIGH: Not being in the middle of a huge mess of monsters and anxiety.

Why would you be in a huge mess of monsters...?

LOW: Uh...that whole part at the beginning of the trip.

HIGH: That amazingly creepy Jack the Ripper tour. They took us to all the good spots!

LOW: Ugh, on the other hand, I finally got to go on the plague tour and it was so weak. We didn't see a single actor in a plague doctor mask. Not a single reenactment of a dying family.

HIGH: How the plague tour <u>wasn't</u> scary!!! Informative and safe!

LOW: Not getting the guards at Buckingham Palace to laugh at us—I really thought we'd do it!

MORE BACKPACKS LOST SINCE LEAVING NEW YORK

1 - left webbed to the back of a double-decker bus that I thought was parked, but was totally in the middle of a tour. Oops.

1 - fell off the gargoyle on the side of Big Ben because that gargoyle was <u>useless.</u>

1 - Flash kicked into the Thames "by accident."

TOTAL BACKPACKS LOST ON TRIP: 11

Aunt May is going to be so mad. She bet Happy that I'd lose fewer than ten backpacks.

LONDON MEMORIES

QUEENS!

HOME, HOME, HOME!

183

I can't believe we made it back to Queens in one piece!

Same. And who knew that we'd come back as such changed men when we started this journal? We were such <u>children</u>.

Ned, it's only been a few weeks. We're still the same age that we were when we left.

Sure, not much actual time has passed, but think about our experiences! We've lived so much.

Okay, quick: Your favorite thing about the trip? Other than Nick Fury. First thing that comes to mind.

PIZZA.

Yeah, we're still kids, buddy.

Fair point.
Being a kid's pretty great, though.

It <u>totally</u> is.

EUROPE BY THE NUMBERS

Who won the trip?

NED DID!

What? Why?

I got more points!

What points? When did we start giving out points?

I've been doing it in my head the whole trip.

AS FAR AS I FIGURE:

Betty Brant as my girlfriend for the trip:
100,000 points

I was right about NY pizza being superior:
1,000 points

Well, then:

I was right about Italian pizza being better:
1,000 points

Defeating a big old evil thing
and saving the world:
1,000,000,000,000 points

That doesn't count! Nothing that
uses spider-powers counts.

Ugh, fine.
The pizza thing, though.

Let's just say we're even and we both won?

That's acceptable, Nedaniel.

Maybe MJ won.
I really like that nickname now.

THE BEST EXCUSES NED CAME UP WITH TO SAVE PETER'S BUTT!

AKA the <u>Only</u> Reason Peter Is <u>Not Expelled</u>

1. He ate something unfortunate and has been in the bathroom <u>all morning</u>.

> I have to admit, this was not my favorite.

2. He's obsessed with Leonardo da Vinci and just <u>had</u> to spend more time in that museum.

> This one actually scored me some points with Mr. Dell!

3. He lost his phone in a gondola and had to sit near the Grand Canal so he could ask every single one that went by whether they had his phone or not.

> Painfully believable. I'm surprised this one didn't happen IRL tbh.

4. We walked by a museum of clowns and he went in and just never came back out! The kid loves clowns. What can I say?

Not cool. Now everyone thinks I love clowns!!

5. He's self-reflecting, Mr. Harrington.

What does that even mean?

I don't know, but I heard Mr. Harrington saying he had to do a lot of it before he could "get back out there" or whatever that means.

I have a good one:

- NUMBER OF BREAKUPS ON THIS TRIP

SPEAKING OF NOT COOL! Peter!!

Kidding!

- NUMBER OF GREAT MEMORIES MADE WITH AWESOME BEST FRIENDS ON THIS TRIP

TOO MANY TO COUNT

Now <u>that</u> I can agree with!

. . . Where are we going next time?

IDK, my arms are still tired from the flight over. BOOM, NED LEEDS OUT WITH A RECYCLED NBJ.

GrROOo
oOOOAA
NnnNnn